KU-074-483

CHICHESTER INSTITUTE OF
HIGHER EDUCATION

WS 2097434 5

AUTHOR

TROUGHTON

TITLE

HOW

CLASS No.

P/TRO

DEC 95

This tale comes from the Tupi Indians of the Amazon in Brazil.
In many stories throughout the world the earth was in the beginning da
but in this myth it is the other way around,
and it is night that is finally set free.

The end papers show a detail from the
decorated fringe of an Indian hammock.

BLACKIE CHILDREN'S BOOKS
Published by the Penguin Group
Penguin Books Ltd, 27 Wrights Lane, London W8 5TZ, England
Penguin Books USA Inc., 375 Hudson Street, New York, New York 10014, USA
Penguin Books Australia Ltd, Ringwood, Victoria, Australia
Penguin Books Canada Ltd, 10 Alcorn Avenue, Toronto, Ontario, Canada M4V 3B2
Penguin Books (NZ) Ltd, 182–190 Wairau Road, Auckland 10, New Zealand

Penguin Books Ltd, Registered Offices: Harmondsworth, Middlesex, England

First published 1986 by Blackie Children's Books
10 9 8 7 6 5 4 3 2 1
This edition first published 1993

Copyright © 1986 Joanna Troughton

The moral right of the author has been asserted

All rights reserved. Without limiting rights under copyright
reserved above, no part of this publication may be reproduced, stored
in or introduced into a retrieval system, or transmitted in any form
or by any means (electronic, mechanical, photocopying, recording or
otherwise), without the prior written permission of both the copyright
owner and the above publisher of this book

Made and printed in Hong Kong

A CIP catalogue record for this book is available from the British Library

ISBN 0–216–91879–0

First American edition published in 1986 by
Peter Bedrick Books
2112 Broadway
New York
NY 10023

Library of Congress Cataloguing-in-
Publication Data
is available for this title
USA ISBN 0-87226–093–3

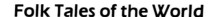

Folk Tales of the World

HOW NIGHT CAME

A Folk Tale from the Amazon

Retold and illustrated by
Joanna Troughton

Blackie
London

Bedrick/Blackie
New York

In the old days there was no night on earth.
It was daylight all the time.
The Great Snake, who ruled the world below
the waters, kept night a prisoner. There were
no animals or birds then, and no fishes in the
river. The forest was quiet.

The daughter of the Great Snake married an Indian and went to live with him on land. But as the days went by she grew ill, and her husband feared for her life.

'It is always daylight here,' she said.

'My eyes are dazzled by the sun. Please ask my father in the world below to send me night, so that I may sleep again.'

So the Indian sent for his three
most trusted servants.

'Go to the Great Snake beneath
the waters,' he said. 'And tell him
that his daughter will die if she has
no sleep. Ask him to set night free.'

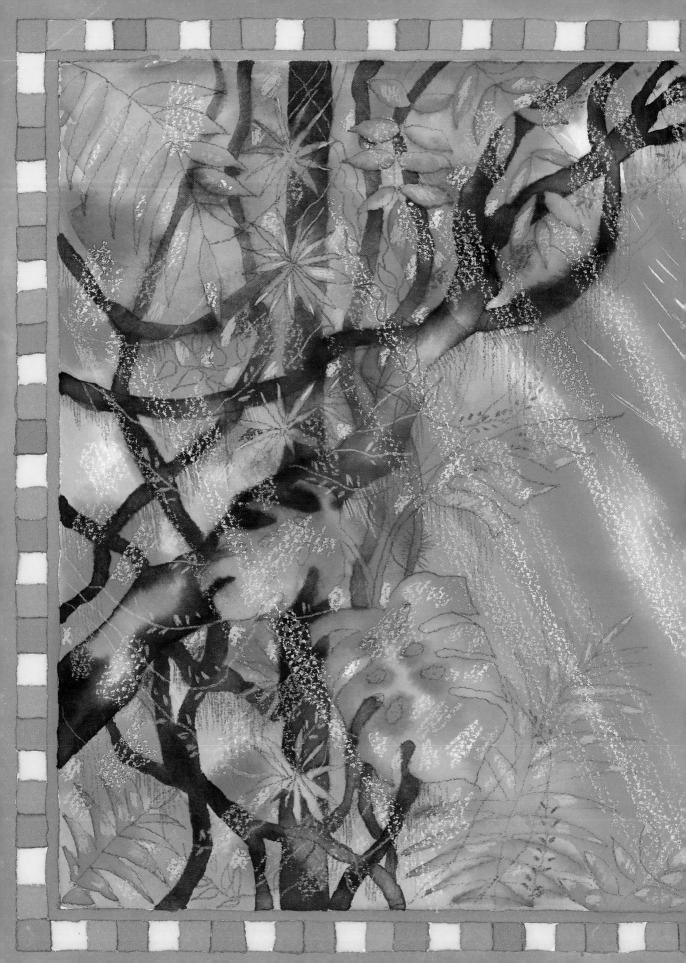

The three trusted servants set out in their canoe.
They paddled to the home of the Great Snake
beneath the waters.

'Your daughter is dying,' the servants told the Great Snake. 'We have been sent to fetch night so that she may sleep.'

When the Great Snake heard their words he took night and placed it in a hollow palm nut which he sealed with resin. 'No one must open this except my daughter,' he told the servants. 'Carry it safely back to her.'

The three trusted servants took the palm nut and paddled back towards land. But as they went they heard strange noises coming from the nut – scratchings, squeakings, croakings and screeching.

The servants were curious. They lit a torch and melted the resin seal. They forgot the warning of the Great Snake and they opened the palm nut.

Night fell . . .

On that first night all the living creatures were made. The sticks in the forest turned into animals.

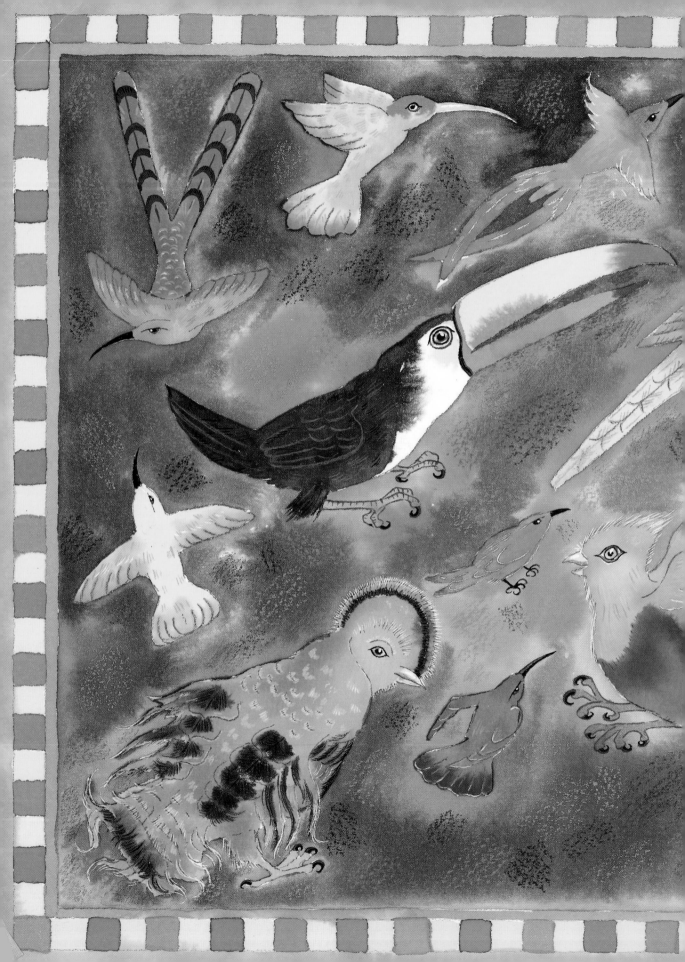

The leaves on the trees turned into birds.

The stones in the river turned into fishes, and
the water weed turned into frogs and snakes.

That night the jaguar was made . . .

. . . the marmoset,
the quetzel and
the humming bird.

The forest was full of the noises of the animals – scratchings, squeakings, croakings and screeching. The three trusted servants had taken no notice of the Great Snake's words, so they were turned into monkeys and went howling from tree to tree.

The daughter of the Great Snake slept at last.
When she awoke it was still night. So she took
two balls of twine and turned them into birds.

'One bird to sing at the beginning of night,
and another to sing at the beginning of day,'
she said.

'Now only half men's lives will be spent in
darkness.'

From that time night has always fallen, but during the day it sleeps beneath the waters.